KAYLENE WINTER

Chapter One

WHY DO FEEL LIKE I'm at my funeral?

Supposedly it's a celebration. A send-off. Some sort of fancy going-away party.

No. It's the end of a fucking era.

The room hums with chatter from the Hungry Lla-ma executive staff—a team my best friend, Austin

Andrews and I put together after we dropped out of college. These are the people who were in the trenches with us for over a decade. Together, we built the company into a gaming unicorn.

Which is now owned by Jacoby International.

They rotate through, clink my glass and say variations of the exact same thing through tight, polished smiles. *"Congrats, dude." "You're gonna be missed." "To new beginnings."*

Almost like memorized lines from a script titled, *How to Toast the Guy Who's Moving On While Everyone Else Stays Put.*

I swirl the whiskey in my glass and take another sip.

This entire evening is surreal. Almost like I'm watching a movie of my life from above. Hell, I'm supposed to be the guest of honor, but I might as well be a corpse in a casket they're all politely circling. I guess everyone wants to have a minute with the departing boss—me.

And then...what?

Fuck it. I take another sip of Midleton and watch Austin with his arm slung around my twin sister Shay. They're laughing at some story one of the accounting team is telling. I'm still coming to terms with the fact they're engaged. They look so damn settled. Comfortable.

Like they've been handed the keys to the rest of their lives and they know exactly what they're doing.

Meanwhile, I sit here smiling and nodding like a jackass while trying to shake the gnawing sense of emptiness permeating my body like a disease.

So here's to "moving on." To "new adventures." To whatever the hell happens next.

But man, even though it's my choice to leave the one job I've ever known, I feel like I've been dumped into some kind of side quest with no map, no mission, and no idea where to go.

Technically, I still have a seat on the board. But sitting in an air-conditioned room full of smug dudes with suits, trying to care about quarterly projections, feels about as exciting as grinding XP in a mobile tower-defense game that's all ads and no payoff.

"Stodge!" Austin's earnest voice cuts through the buzz. He holds up two glasses of champagne, grinning like a damn idiot. "We're toasting! Get over here."

Like I have a choice. I run a hand through my hair as I cross the room and take my place by his side. The whiskey's warm in my chest, but not enough to dull the nagging feeling I'm coasting while everyone else is leveling up.

"To Miles Stojanović a.k.a. '*Stodge.*'" Austin slings his arm around my shoulder, dragging me into the small circle with Shay. "Visionary. Creative genius. The heart of Hungry Llama. We couldn't have done this without you."

I dutifully clink my glass against his and then tap it to my sister's. "Couldn't have done it without you, bro." I force a grin, meeting Shay's eyes for a second.

She smiles brightly, but her gaze is soft. She knows. Of course, she does. We're twins, after all.

Austin is still yammering on about me and something about he and I being a team forever. Blah blah blah. The words are fine and the sentiment's nice, but all I can think about is how forever looks different now. Austin has Shay, Hungry Llama has a new owner, and I have…

Nothing.

No, scratch that. I have money. A stupid amount of money. Enough to burn through a hundred lifetimes of bad decisions and still be fine. Enough to make me invisible if I don't want to flash my credentials. But what's the point of any of it if I'm filled with this weird emptiness?

Like everything I've worked for is for nothing. Because I'm alone. I've given Hungry Llama my heart. My soul. My youth.

I guess I thought being rich would be worth it.

It's not.

Shay sticks close and gathers me into a hug when the toasts die down. "You okay?" she asks quietly, her chin tilted so Austin can't hear.

"Yeah," I lie.

Her brow furrows, but she doesn't push. I don't want her to because as the time of the party winds down, I've made up my mind.

It's time for me to find my fucking joy.

The Uber drops me off at my sleek high-rise in downtown Seattle. I never got around to furnishing it properly but I have some basics so it's not totally empty. I kick off my sneakers, pour a glass of Gatorade Zero, and sit on a barstool at my kitchen island.

I click on Kayak and search for first-class flights to Europe.

The results populate. Rome. Madrid. Berlin. Paris.

Paris catches my eye. Always does. Austin and I went there once for a gaming conference when we launched our company and were traveling on the cheap. Back then, he and I were two geeks chasing an impossible dream. We had six hours of free time before our flight left and spent most of it getting lost on the cobblestone streets, filling our bellies with pastries and laughing at ourselves for butchering the language.

We often reminisced about how we'd go back and do it up once we "made" it. Neither of us bothered, though. Too caught up in the day-to-day of running a billion-dollar company, and the opportunity never presented itself.

In any case, I pick Paris. Who doesn't love Paris?

I don't overthink it. I book the ticket, grab a carry-on, and toss in some basic clothes, figuring I can do laundry or buy what I need. My passport's in my dresser drawer, a little dusty but still valid. By midnight, I'm packed and ready for my early flight.

The flight's relaxing. I eat the surprisingly delicious first-class airline meal. Drink a couple of glasses of whiskey. Adjust my seat into lie-flat mode and let the background hum of engines lull me into a fairly restful sleep.

By the time my plane lands at Charles de Gaulle, it's already early evening. Customs is a breeze and before I know it, I'm squinting against the fluorescent lights and following signs to the RER train.

I don't have a plan. That's the point.

An hour later, I'm standing in front of a fancy five-star hotel in the Marais district with wrought-iron balconies and flower boxes spilling over with red geraniums. Charming as hell—and it has availability. I drop my bag in the room, splash some water on my face, and change into something less crumpled.

Stepping out into the Parisian night, I have no idea what I'm looking for.

But, I'm already itching to find it.

Chapter Two

Paris isn't doing its job.

For God's sake, it's supposed to feel like home.

I was born here. I'm fluent in the language. My mother, Parisian to her core, always tells me this city is in my blood. This city has a magic I'll always carry with me.

Tonight, unfortunately, I feel about as magical as a tax return.

I'm perched on a bar stool, alone at a wine bar called Magnum La Cave, which is tucked off a main drag in Marais, a couple blocks away from my hotel. The place leans hard into its name with walls covered in photos of a mustachioed Tom Selleck from the 80s-era *Magnum PI* show.

Somehow—against all odds—it's not tacky, but charming. The place is popular and the buzz from the tables outside spills into the cozy, character-packed interior, where I swirl my glass of Bordeaux and watch the people around me. A group of women shriek with laughter and clink their glasses together. Two men in suits dig into a gorgeous plate of cheese and charcuterie. Next to me, an older couple leans in close, speaking quietly before sharing a sweet kiss.

Closing my eyes, I sigh deeply and take a large sip of wine. Not because I begrudge them.

If anything, I envy them.

I want what they have.

Instead, I'm thirty-two, single, sitting in Paris trying to remember what it felt like to be wanted. Worshipped. Adored.

Mark was supposed to be the one. We met in our twenties, two young go-getters carving out our glamorous life in New York. I was the artistic one, dreaming of making a living taking photographs. He was practical, with a steady accounting job and great income.

We balanced each other, or so I thought. He kept me from flying off in too many directions at once. I brought some fun into his life. Over time, steady turned into critical, grounded turned into dismissive, and by the time I was finding success in my career, he was busy tearing me down.

"I just don't see why you care so much," he scoffed when I booked a major campaign with Valentino. *"It's just fashion photography, Sophie. You're not curing cancer."*

I convinced myself he'd come around as soon as my work received critical recognition. Seven years later, I was the most-coveted photographer in fashion and I'd won several awards. Yet, I was still waiting for some acknowledgement by Mark telling me my career was worthwhile.

Meanwhile, he was offered his dream job—the CFO at an international bank. We'd both made it, so I figured I might as well stay. We'd been together so long, why throw it all away? Marriage, the house, the family. It was the next step.

We even picked out a place. A fixer-upper brownstone in Brooklyn, which was a little overpriced but perfect. The wide windows in one of the bedrooms made it a perfect studio. The third bedroom I dreamed of filling with a crib.

Two days before we were supposed to move in, Mark blindsided me.

"I've decided not to move in. I'm not happy, Sophie," he said over gnocchi at our favorite Italian restaurant. "You're not either. Why are we pretending?"

I remember staring at him, unable to speak. My prime childbearing years were slipping away and I'd been holding out for something he'd given up on. And the worst part? He wasn't wrong.

Six months later and the brownstone's mine. I can afford it—thank God my career is thriving—but it wasn't supposed to be like this. We were supposed to fill it with love. Babies. A future.

I'm still picking up the pieces.

Taking a sip of wine, I glance at my phone. The email I received an hour ago fills my screen. Confirmation of my first solo exhibit at the Carmichael Gallery. Thirty-five pieces. An exhibit signifying a culmination of years of work and fighting for respect in an industry where photographers are seen as disposable—hell, Mark sure did.

It's everything I've wanted. And yet, I can't even muster up an ounce of enthusiasm.

The door to the bar swings open and an unexpected gust of cool air makes me glance up.

Holy fuck.

The man who walks in is tall and broad-shouldered with dirty-blond hair falling in loose, messy waves. His leather jacket looks well-loved, like he's had it since he was a teenager. Underneath the coat he wears a black t-shirt tucked into faded jeans and lopes in with an easy stride. He seems youthful and uncalculated.

He pauses just inside the doorway, scanning the room like he's not certain where to go. His gaze brushes over me briefly before moving on, but there's something in the way he carries himself. I want to keep watching him.

He's magnetic. Not in a polished, cocky way. There's a softness to him. Something accessible and curious, like he hasn't figured out how the world works but isn't too worried about it.

Jesus. What's wrong with me?

I look down at my near-empty glass, embarrassed at my reaction to a stranger. I didn't come here to pick up some random guy. I'm in Paris because I just finished shooting Fashion Week. I'm staying for a few weeks to figure out my life. The last thing I need is to ogle some random guy.

I'm here for the kind of introspection that'll only happen when I'm shopping on ancient cobblestone streets, indulging in spa days and drinking overpriced wine.

Alone.

Suddenly, he's at the bar an armlength away. He orders something—I can't hear what—and shifts just slightly to glance back around the room while he waits. His eyes catch mine again for a moment and holy hell. My heart actually stutters.

I look away, heat rises in my cheeks. I'm positive everyone in this room can see my reaction to him.

Ugh.

Do. Not. Make. Eye. Contact.

Bending over, I adjust my camera bag on the back of my chair and pretend to check my phone. Anything to avoid looking at him again. Out of the corner of my eye, I get a glimpse of him, drink in hand, heading toward the empty seat next to me.

No. Nope. Not tonight.

I reach for my glass, intending to finish it swiftly and leave. In my fumbling rush, I knock it over instead.

"Shit!" The wine splashes everywhere and a streak of dark red spreads across the bar, pooling onto the floor. Mortified, I grab a tiny bar napkin and feverishly blot at the mess.

"Need a hand?" a deep voice drawls.

I freeze.

It's him. Standing there. Holding a full glass of wine in one hand and perusing the chaos with an amused smile.

"No, it's fine." My cheeks burn as I keep blotting with my soaked little square of paper. "Really, it's nothing."

"Oh, it's something." He sets his glass down, grabs a handful of napkins from the bar and kneels down to wipe up the floor. "But hey, I shouldn't judge. Last week, I dropped an entire iced coffee in the middle of Starbucks."

Despite myself, I laugh.

His grin widens, boyish and charming, and for the first time tonight, I feel my shoulders relax.

"Thanks." I allow myself to look at him directly.

He tosses the soaked napkins into a trash can at the end of bar and takes the seat next to me. "You're welcome. Do you spill drinks often or am I just the lucky guy who gets to use it as an excuse to meet you?"

"You caught me. It was a tactical spill," I deadpan. The corners of my mouth twitch despite my best effort to stay composed. "I figured causing a scene might summon a hero—looks like it worked."

"Well, here I am." He laughs, light and teasing. There's something genuine in his eyes. "I'll try not to disappoint."

For a second, I take him in. He's so sweet. Earnest. Hot as fuck.

This isn't part of the plan.

But here we are.

Something tells me I'm not walking out of this bar as the same person who walked in.

Chapter Three

JET LAG IS NO joke.

It's day two—well, night two. My body's screaming for sleep, but my brain won't stop buzzing.

After I checked in, I dined alone at a little bistro where I enjoyed a stellar meal of steak frites. I even drank an entire bottle of wine, figuring it would help me sleep. But, no. I lay awake all fucking night long staring at the ceiling, finally passing out around breakfast time after I rubbed one out.

When I woke up it was midafternoon. Now I'm in the twilight zone of being exhausted but also wired. For the past several hours, I've walked half the Marais trying to shake off this annoying restless energy.

It's not working.

God, I'm finding it impossible to relax. It feels like I'm forgetting to do something. Years of deadlines, product launches, and running a business has messed me up. I have no idea how to chill anymore.

Which fucking sucks.

Plus, I've come to the realization my spur-of-the-moment decision to hop on a plane might not have been the most-well-thought-out plan. I don't speak French. I know exactly zero people here. I'm too old for nightclubs, too restless to sit alone in a café, and bars aren't my thing.

I'm standing there, debating whether to wander aimlessly or admit defeat and go back to the hotel when I spot it—a wine bar tucked into a quiet corner, glowing with warm, golden light.

Magnum. The name's printed on the awning in clean, sharp lettering. Tables spill out onto the street, lively but not chaotic. Inside, it looks...perfect. Busy, but not overly crowded. Doesn't seem pretentious.

Stepping inside, I immediately love the vibe—the perfect mix of cozy and cool. Soft chatter hums under the faint clink of glasses. The décor is quirky and eclectic—photos of Tom Selleck in full *Magnum PI* glory line the walls, for God's sake. How could you go wrong?

This'll work. At least for tonight.

I scan the room and see *her*.

The woman seems to be alone, elbow resting on the bar as she swirls the final bit of red wine in her glass. She's stunning in a undeniably effortless way. Dark, chestnut hair is swept back in a large clip. Loose strands brush her cheekbones. Her skin glows under the warm light, and her eyes—green, intense—flick around the room like she's studying it. She wears a simple black dress with a colorful scarf draped around her shoulders.

I don't know what it is about her. It takes every ounce of self-control not to stare.

Crossing the room toward the bar, I order a glass of red wine, leaving it up to the bartender to choose for me. I lean against the counter as I wait. Out of the corner of my eye, I see her dig for something in a bag slung across the back of her stool. She fumbles slightly, her hand brushing the stem—and suddenly, the wine tips.

It's like slow motion. The red liquid spills across the table, dripping over the edge and pooling on the floor. She mutters something under her breath and grabs one of those tiny bar napkins, blotting furiously at the mess.

Before I can stop myself, I grab a fistful of bar napkins and step forward. "Need a hand?"

She stops for a second, like I've startled her. When she looks up, I notice two things: her cheeks are flushed, and her eyes are sharp, sizing me up like she's not convinced I'm actually here to help.

"No, it's fine." Her voice is tight but controlled. "Really, it's nothing."

"Oh, it's something," I smile as I crouch to wipe up the floor. "But hey, I shouldn't judge. Last week, I dropped an entire iced coffee in the middle of Starbucks."

To my surprise, she laughs softly and she seems to relax a bit. "Thanks." She finally looks me in the eye, and holy hell. I've never seen a more beautiful woman in my life.

"You're welcome." I toss the wet napkins in the trash and take the seat next to her. "Do you spill drinks often or am I just the lucky guy who gets to use it as an excuse to meet you?"

Her lips twitch, and for a second, I think she might actually smile. "You caught me. It was a tactical spill." Her dry sense of humor catches me off guard. "I figured causing a scene might summon a hero—looks like it worked."

"Well, here I am." I laugh heartily. "I'll try not to disappoint."

For a moment, neither of us says anything. She studies me like she's still deciding whether or not I'm worth talking to. I wait with baited breath, hoping for a miracle.

"Do you always rescue strangers?" Her fingernail digs at the wood on the bar top.

"Only if they have excellent taste in wine." I gesture to the bottle of Bordeaux sitting next to her overturned glass. My cheesy line garners a genuine smile—a small one, but it's there. I offer my hand. "Miles."

She takes it and her grip is firm. "Sophie."

"*Sophie*," I repeat. Her name rolls off my tongue. It suits her—effortless, classic, and a little intriguing.

Sophie picks up her glass and refills it, taking a small sip. Her gaze flicks back to me. "So, what brings you to Paris?"

The question feels loaded somehow. I debate giving her the short answer, but something about her makes me want to be honest.

"I needed a change," I say finally. "I just sold my company—a gaming studio I started with my best friend. Now I'm figuring out what's next."

Her eyebrows lift slightly, as though she's intrigued. "Gaming studio?"

"Hungry Llama." I brace for the inevitable blank stare.

Instead, her lips curve into a smile. "Oh, how cool. My niece loves *Puzzle Pet Paradise*. She spent last Christmas trying to explain it to me."

"Clearly, she's a genius." I nod solemnly. "And you should listen to her."

She rolls her eyes, but there's warmth there. "What's it like? Selling a business you built from scratch?"

"It's...weird," I admit. "I *should* feel excited, but mostly I feel like I'm floating. I spent so much time building the company, growing it. Running it. I forgot to think about what happens after."

For a moment, she just watches me, her expression unreadable. "I get it." She nods. "The in-between."

"What about you? What brings you here?" I finish my glass of wine.

Sophie pours me another glass from her bottle, then her gaze drops. "I'm a photographer. I just finished shooting Fashion Week, now I'm taking a few weeks to...figure things out."

"Figure what out?" I tilt my head to the side. Talking to her feels effortless. Like we're old friends catching up.

She hesitates, and for a second, I think she's going to brush it off. But then she sighs as her fingers trace the rim of her glass.

"Tonight I found out something pretty cool. I've been offered a solo exhibit." She closes her eyes and smiles, then catches herself and resumes a reserved demeanor. "In New York this fall. It's a big deal—huge, actually. Instead of being excited, I feel, *um*. Untethered."

Her honesty surprises me. It's refreshing. Raw. Something about her demeanor provides me with a surge of kinship. It's strange, but also comforting.

"Hmmm. Maybe untethered is normal for people like us," I hear myself say.

Her eyebrow spikes. "People like *us*?"

"Yeah. People who create things." My words roll off my tongue effortlessly. "We're artists."

My words linger in the air and I can't help but realize I've never spoken my truth out loud. It's both confusing and exhilarating. Sophie catches on because her expression thoroughly softens.

For the rest of the evening, our conversation flows easily. Like we've known each other our whole lives. We talk about New York and Seattle. Why we're in Paris and about the strange pull of ambition and the toll it takes.

I tell her about how lost I am without my company and the loneliness I'm feeling because my sister is marrying my best friend. How I have no idea what my next step is. She confides the details of her devastating breakup and how she's leaving in a couple days to visit her parents in Bordeaux—to complete her healing process in the care of the people who love her most.

Long ago, the hum of the bar faded into the background. It's just the two of us now, leaning slightly toward each other, wine glasses in hand. The space between us grows smaller with every passing minute.

I can't recall ever having a connection to someone so suddenly. So easily. Like fate guided us both to this strange little wine bar at the exact same time so we could meet.

When Magnum eventually closes, we walk slowly down *Rue Beautreillis* toward the Seine. Sophie points out a building where Jim Morrison, the singer of the 60s band the Doors died. Apparently it's a famous landmark, though I've never heard of him.

We turn onto *Quai des Célestins*, falling into an easy rhythm as we continue our conversation. On our stroll, we continue to chat about everything and nothing. A discussion about *Stranger Things* turns into a story about how she navigated straddling two cultures. I tell her about my twin sister and how difficult it was to be the quiet, shy computer nerd compared to the outgoing, opinionated beauty queen.

Sophie and I marvel at how similar our stories are. Both of us have cool careers most people only dream of—her capturing fleeting moments through a camera lens, me building a digital world pixel by pixel.

We stop at the railing for a moment. The river shimmers in the golden light of the overhead street lamps. I steal a glance as she gazes out at the water, her face serene and peaceful.

I know, with certainty, I don't want this night to end.

"This has been…" I pause, searching for the suitable words. "I don't know—one of those meetings you don't ever plan for. But, uh…" I gesture vaguely behind me. "I just realized my hotel is a block away."

She turns to face me, her lips curve up slightly. "Oh yeah?"

I kick the ground with my toe, feeling a little foolish. I hope she doesn't think I'm a player. "I'm staying at—"

"*Cheval Blanc*," we both say at the exact time.

There's a beat of silence, then she bursts out laughing. A rich, melodic sound making my chest feel lighter.

"You're kidding." I shake my head.

Sophie's eyes sparkle with amusement. "What are the odds we'd booked the same five-star hotel."

"Apparently, decent enough." I chuckle. "I think Paris had some grand plan for us to meet."

She tilts her head. "Or, maybe, we're both ridiculously lucky."

"Could be," I admit with a smirk.

The coincidence settles between us, equal parts absurd and perfect.

And right. Oh, so right.

Chapter Four

My heart isn't just pounding—it's tap dancing, leaping, spinning in ways both ridiculous and undeniable.

I can't remember a time where I felt...this on edge.

It's not just excitement; it's like the second you step onto a tightrope, high above the city, knowing something extraordinary is waiting on the other side.

Though, to be fair, I haven't walked on any tightropes lately.

Or *ever*.

The night door man Lucien's face lights up as we approach the doors of *Cheval Blanc*.

"Mademoiselle Dumond", he greets me warmly, his French accent rich and familiar. *"Bon retour, avez-vous passé une bonne soirée?"*

"Bonsoir, Lucien. Oui, une très belle soirée, merci". I smile, catching Miles's confusion as his eyes ping-pong between us. Clearly, he doesn't speak French.

Cheval Blanc has been my Parisian retreat for years. I've spent countless nights here during Fashion Week, photoshoots, and other visits to my favorite city. It's renowned for impeccable service. Every member of the staff remembers your name, your favorite table, even your preferred vintage of wine.

Miles slows, his gaze sweeping over the lobby. The patterned stone floors gleam under the light, the towering contemporary Eiffel Tower sculpture commands attention, and the golden screens shimmer like something out of an interior designer's dream. "I can't get over how incredible this place is," he murmurs quietly, almost to himself.

"It's my favorite hotel in the world." I rock back on my heels giddily. "It's my home base every time I'm in Paris. I take it this is your first time staying here?"

"Uh, yeah. I'm used to pretty utilitarian hotels. I could get used to the fancy things, though." He looks a little uncomfortable, like he's not positive where the evening is going to take us.

I hesitate slightly but start toward the front desk. "Should we see about a bottle of wine, or are you tired?"

"I could drink more wine. I was *hoping* we could hang out for a while." A huge smile spreads across his face as we approach the hotel clerk.

"Mademoiselle Dumond, toujours un plaisir," she says before turning to Miles and switching to English. "And *Monsieur* Stojanović, welcome back to Cheval Blanc. How may we assist you this evening?"

Miles leans closer to me, raising an eyebrow. "Do they know every guest by name?"

"Only the important ones," I tease.

"Important, huh?" He turns back to the concierge. "We were wondering if there's somewhere we could sit and have a nightcap?"

Her expression softens apologetically. "Regretfully, our bars and restaurants have closed for the evening.

However, we would be delighted to send a bottle of champagne and some light bites to the rooftop terrace. The view is particularly stunning tonight."

Miles looks at me and quirks an eyebrow.

"Sounds perfect. *Merci.*' I nod toward the elevator. "Should we go up?'

The terrace is breathtaking. Paris stretches out before us, a glittering sea of light and shadow. The Eiffel Tower glows like a beacon, its reflection sparkles in the Seine below. When the champagne and hors d'oeuvres arrive, Miles pours us each a glass, handing one to me with a little flourish.

"To tactical spills." He raises his glass.

"To shared hotels," I counter, beaming as our glasses clink.

We sink into the plush chairs. The champagne is crisp and bright on my tongue. At just past midnight, it's quiet except for the distant hum of the city. Our conversation continues to flow as easily as the bubbly.

"So, have you always been this lucky?" I gesture to the view with my champagne glass. It's been such a surreal evening.

Miles blushes slightly. "Hardly. A city this glamorous is usually my sister's scene, not mine. I've spent most of my life in Seattle. Work, the occasional snowboard trip, rinse, repeat."

"So...Seattle," I echo. "I forgot to mention I was there once for a shoot. Beautiful town. Very...moody."

He nods. "It is. But I've always dreamed about traveling for pleasure, you know? Seeing the world when I'm not in some big conference hall at a gaming convention. I've never had the time before."

"And now?" I tilt my head, intrigued.

"Now," he smirks, "I'm here, on a rooftop in Paris, drinking champagne with a beautiful, intelligent, witty woman who has excellent taste in hotels."

I throw my head back and laugh. God. This guy. I've never had such an effortless conversation in my life.

"What about you? Have you always lived in New York?" He leans back and turns toward me.

"Mostly." I curl my legs under me and face him. "I do travel a lot for work—Europe, Asia, a little bit of everywhere. New York is home, though. For now."

"For now?" His eyes catch mine and hold.

I hesitate, but don't look away. "Sometimes I wonder if I'm too rooted there. My career's there, my brownstone's there... I've always dreamed about doing something different, though. Traveling. Maybe starting a travel and photography blog. I also want a family, and I'm not getting any younger."

"It's not unrealistic." Miles shakes his head. "Scary. But not unrealistic."

There's something in his voice—earnest, certain—that makes me believe him.

As the night deepens, our conversation drifts into stories about the past, the little details shaping who we are today.

"It's funny." Miles relaxes back. "My twin sister, Shay, is my biggest inspiration. She's been through so much—living with epilepsy, figuring out how to live on her terms—and now, with Austin, it's like she's found this perfect balance. They've got their whole world together which is—different for me. I need to figure out who I am outside of being Austin's business partner or Shay's brother." He glances at me, his expression sincere and unguarded. "I guess I'm a cliche. I'm in Paris to find myself."

I suck in a breath as his words sink in. "I get it. I thought Mark and I were building a life together. Looking back, I was the only one trying." I hesitate, then add, "He never supported my work. Treated it like a phase. And I let him, because I wanted the family, the future I'd imagined. Then one night, before we were supposed to move into a new place, he ended it. Said we weren't happy anymore." I glance at the skyline, then back at Miles. "He wasn't wrong. And now I'm here, trying to figure out who I am on my own."

For a moment, neither of us speaks. The weight of our confessions hang in the air.

Then Miles leans forward slightly, his voice low but certain. "Sounds like you're already doing it."

"As are you." I let out the breath I've been holding.

The champagne is almost gone, we're both a bit drunk and I'm caught in a dilemma. I want to spend the night with Miles. Does he feel how I do?

Meeting you feels like a movie." I look out at the Eiffel Tower after I say the words. Truthfully? I'm too out of practice to take charge.

Miles leans toward me, his movement unhurried, as if he's giving this moment space to breathe. "The *best* movie."

I glance at him, wondering if this is what it feels like to find exactly what you didn't know you were looking for.

When his lips meet mine, it's like the world tilts on its axis. Our kiss is warm and electric. Soft with a quiet intensity.

I'm breathless.

In a moment that categorically rewrites everything before it.

Chapter Five

Her lips are still warm on mine when the kiss ends.

Yet, I can still feel her—like her presence has sunk beneath my skin, leaving me branded.

For a moment, we stay like this. Still. Her hand rests lightly on my chest, her lips just a breath away from mine, and I'm clutching her waist like letting go might send her spiraling out of range.

It's overwhelming—this feeling. The pull. The need to be closer to her even though we've just met. It's absurd. I barely know her. And yet, without a shadow of doubt, it's clear the moment I walked into Magnum tonight I was always going to end up here with her.

I should say something. Anything. But the words won't come and, for now, maybe it's okay. It's enough to stay rooted here, caught in this strange, undeniable gravity pulling us together, something far bigger than we are.

Sophie leans back just enough to look at me. Her gaze feels like a spotlight and an invitation all at once. For a split second, I forget how to breathe.

"Well." I find my voice, trying to break the spell without shattering it. "That was…"

"Unexpected?" She seems hesitant.

I grip her face gently in my palms. "I was going to say inevitable."

The words hang between us. Her lips twitch and curve into the faintest smile, and it makes my heart do something reckless in my chest—like it's daring me to leap, to trust this moment, to see where it leads.

Her fingers comb through my hair. The movement is casual, but her eyes stay locked on mine, unblinking, unshaken.

"I guess I should say goodnight." She casts her eyes downward then back up at me. There's no finality in her tone. It's a statement waiting for an answer, a question disguised as certainty.

"You could," I drawl, the words thick with the weight of everything I want to say but don't.

She bites her lip. "But?"

"But...I don't think either of us wants to say goodnight." I lean forward to close some of the space between us.

For a moment time stands still. She looks at me. Vulnerable. Like she's examining my motive. Finally, she lets out a quiet, almost breathless laugh and the tension snaps, shifting into something warmer. Deeper.

Undeniable.

"You're dangerous, Miles," she murmurs. The way she says my name sends a thrill down my spine.

I shake my head. "Uh, *no*. I think you might be the dangerous one."

"Walk me to my room?" She stands. Slow and deliberate. Her movements as graceful as they are decisive.

Her question hits like a bolt of lightning.

Jolted, I rise and take Sophie's hand as we step away from the table, our touch light and fleeting, but enough to send my pulse skittering. "Lead the way."

Threaded with anticipation, the elevator ride feels like a heartbeat stretched across infinity. We stare at each other. Neither of us says anything, but the air is thick with unspoken words.

I'm dying to pull her closer, but I wait. Let the tension grow. Let it simmer.

When the elevator doors open and we step into the hallway, the silence isn't awkward—it's charged. Every step feels deliberate, like we're crossing a threshold the universe knew we'd pass through eventually.

We arrive at her door and she turns to me, her lips parting slightly as if to say something, but I don't let her. I can't wait a minute longer.

My hands span her waist and I kiss her again, deeper this time. She responds instantly, her fingers curling into the front of my shirt as she pulls me closer. Our kiss is a slow burn, unraveling everything between us, and I feel her smile against my lips, like she's daring me to lose control.

"Sophie," I murmur, her name a quiet reverence.

She grips my forearms. "Stay."

The word hangs in the air between us. A challenge and an invitation all at once.

"Are you certain?" I ask softly, barely able to believe this is happening.

"You're sweet," she says huskily. "But I think we both know the answer."

And just like that, the question is settled. The door opens and our mouths crash together the minute we step inside. Her tongue rubs against mine in a slow, sexy tease. For now, I'm happy to let Sophie take the lead, and to my delight, there's no hesitation whatsoever.

She nips my lower lip, sinking in her teeth, which sends a streak of need straight to my cock. My tongue pursues hers, twining and twisting while my hips press against her core. I grasp her cheeks and turn her head to where I want her. Pushing her further because somehow, I instinctively know she needs me to make her feel wanted.

I'm the man for the job because I've never wanted anyone the way I do Sophie.

Sophie meets my kisses with urgent lips. Her hands frantically slide along my back, on my chest, settling on my neck, where she threads her fingers through my too-long hair. What's happening between us is pure, primal need.

When I can't take any more, I draw back and haul in a deep breath. Her eyes remain closed, dark lashes against her flushed, pink cheeks. She's stunning. Her high cheekbones. The delicate arch of her eyebrows. Her mouth. God, her mouth. Unable to stop myself, I take it again using my thumb to tilt her up to meet my lips.

"Look at me," I whisper into her mouth. "Show me you know who's in this bedroom with you."

Sophie blinks up at me, her eyes hazy and unfocused. I shed my coat and rip off my t-shirt and fall to my knees before her, palms on her hips. Nuzzling her belly, I allow my hands to roam back to her ass to drag her closer. I kiss down her stomach to the vee of her thighs and breathe in her arousal.

I have to taste her.

Looking up, I find Sophie watching me as I drag the hem of her dress up her thighs. I stop for a moment and she nods her assent, so I continue until I've gathered the material at her waist. With my free hand, my fingers slip under the silky fabric of her panties and swipe along her swollen slit.

"Oh, hell," she chokes out, and with a lash of my tongue against her clit, she stills. Moans, low and keening.

Her knees buckle and she nearly falls to the ground, but I manage to catch her with an arm behind her thighs. I slant my head to suck on her lower lips and dart my tongue through her juices. She cups my head in her hands and subtly directs me to where she needs me to be. Swivels her ass in slow, erotic circles as the tip of my tongue probes every millimeter of her wet folds.

Finally, I capture her clit and suck, increasing the pressure when cries out and her thighs begin to shake.

"Please. Make me come." Sophie sounds so throaty—so aroused, I nearly come in my jeans.

"Oh, I'll get you there, baby. Don't worry." I rise, and in a bout of confidence, lift her and toss her onto the bed.

Surprised but game, Sophie scrambles back against the pillows, leans up on her elbows, pulls up her dress and spreads her legs. I don't hesitate, I lower myself between them and yank off her panties.

Her glistening pussy is like a beautiful pink flower. One I'm going to devour. I drag my tongue from bottom to top and wrap my hands around her thighs, opening her wide. Fisting the sheets, she undulates under me as I savor every swipe, nip, lick and suck.

I feel her building, and all I want is for her to shatter. I flick my tongue back and forth against her clit, desperate for the taste of her release. She pulses with each swipe, her ass grinding futilely into the mattress. Pressing my hand against her mound, I pinch her lips together as I wiggle my tongue around her little nub.

"Shit. Oh God," she moans. "Miles, please don't stop."

Her thighs tighten around my ears, trapping me in her silky heat. I slide a finger inside, crooking it against her spongy little area causing her to bow up. "You're wound so tight, Sophie. You need to come so bad, don't you?"

"Yes." She throws back her head and frantically pinches at her nipples through the bodice of her dress. "I need it."

"I need it too." It's true. I know I'll die if I don't give her the best orgasm of her life.

I slide my finger inside and out, adding a second, then a third. My dick is trying to burrow out of my jeans, but so what. This is all about her. Her pussy is visibly quivering, puffy folds squeezing against my digits. I close my lips around her clit, sucking and thrusting in rhythm until she bucks wildly and grips my hair, pulling my face deeper into her delicious inferno.

Her entire body ripples and I drink down every drop, soothing her through the aftermath until her thighs splay on the bed and she lets out the breath she's been holding this entire time.

"Wow you're a master at...at... This...*ahhhh*." Sophie flings an arm over her eyes and smiles.

"Going down on you is the first course." I kiss my way up her stomach until we're face to face, and push her arm up so I can see her beautiful eyes. "We're just getting started."

Before I allow myself a wink of sleep, I'm going to explore every inch of Sophie's beautiful body.

Count on it.

Chapter Six

Miles presses his mouth to mine.

His kiss consumes me, deep and deliberate, like he's been waiting his whole life for this moment.

It's not just a kiss—it's a fire, a pull so intense it leaves me trembling, undone. No one has ever kissed me like this. With this much hunger. This much need.

Like I'm the only woman who exists in his world. It's overwhelming. And, I don't want it to stop.

Moaning, I thrust my hands into his hair, slashing my tongue against his. We go at each other for what feels like hours until he draws back from my mouth. "I need to be inside you, Sophie."

God. I can't wait. "Yes. Yes. Hurry."

I manage to loosen my hair, which spills down over my shoulder as he pulls the zipper of my dress down my back. I sit up, holding it against my breasts, watching as he goes to work on the buttons of his jeans. When he stands before me in a pair of boxer briefs, I lower my arm and let the bodice fall to my waist.

"Damn." He rests one knee on the bed next to me, staring at my distended nipples through my sheer black bra. I flick the clasp between my breasts and the cups fall away, baring them to him. He reaches out and thumbs each taut peak one after the other and looks into my eyes. "You're the most stunning woman I've ever seen."

Here we are in Paris. Naked in my hotel room. Strangers. No, friends. Meh...a vacation fling.

Or, *maybe*, soul mates.

All I know is it's time. "Fuck me, Miles."

"Yes, ma'am." Miles grins and nips my bare shoulder and bends down to grab his wallet from his jeans.

I dare a glance at the tent in his underwear and hiss out a breath as I clamp my palm around his length. "You're huge."

"Sophie." He grabs me around the waist with one arm and tugs me backward, causing me to release my grip. Bites my earlobe, playfully. "Let it be known, I'm not gonna fuck you until you beg for my cock. *Plead* for it. Meanwhile, I'll just keep doing this—" he pinches my nipples one by one then swipes a finger along my slit "—while you get wetter and wetter."

His smutty talk has me gushing, but what he doesn't realize is there's a dirty girl inside me raging to get out and I want Miles to unlock my cage. Swiftly, my hand dives under the waistband of his briefs and grips his thick shaft, thumbing the wetness over the tip. "Maybe I'll make you beg too."

Miles laughs. "Touché."

"Lots of talk. No action yet," I taunt.

He leans over to suck on the side of my neck and plunges his fingers inside me all the way to the hilt. "Okay miss lippy-pants. Let's get back to the action." He finds the spot that drove me wild earlier and strokes. "You're so tight and wet around me. I think you were made for my cock."

"Ahhhhhhh," I quiver-moan as he grazes his teeth down the line of my throat, still managing to stroke him up and down.

"Tell me what you want. Use your words." Miles bucks into my hand frantically.

"I want your cock in me. Deep and hard." The words burst out of me in a torrent. "I want you to fuck me so hard I scream. I want the people in the next building to know how good I'm being fucked. I want to let go for once. Know what it's like to be free."

Once I admit my most carnal desire, I feel a rush of heat climb my neck and I almost pull back, folding into myself, embarrassed for daring to ask for so much from a man I just met.

Too much.

Miles tilts my face up to his with his free hand, eyes blazing so intensely, it steals away my breath. "Sophie," he says, low and anguished, "stay with me in this moment. Don't ever shy away from asking for everything you deserve. I swear, if you let me, I'll give you anything you need."

I nod, unable to speak. Unable to believe how this night is unfolding.

Miles grabs the condom he retrieved from his jeans and tears it open, rolling it down his shaft. He positions himself between my legs on his knees and fists his cock, flicking it through my folds. "Guide me home. Put me in you."

"Okay." I look down and place my hand over his, showing him how I like it. Together we watch as I run the tip of his cock through my swollen lips. Drag him through the slick trails of my arousal. Place him at my entrance and take him all the way in with one roll of my hips.

It's the hottest thing I've ever done.

"God." Miles squeezes his eyes shut. "Don't move, baby. Let me feel you like this for a minute."

We stay like this for a few seconds before I grip his forearms, which are braced on either side of my head. "Please move," I purr. "I need it."

"Yeah, okay. I've got control now." He bites his lips and thrusts all the way in. Slowly. Then does it again. "You feel...*ahhhhh*."

I tilt my ass up to receive him. "Faster, Miles. Please. Fuck me."

My words seem to scorch a path of lightning through his entire being. He grips my hips and pulls all the way out, hovering with just his tip inside while I shiver with anticipation. He sinks in slow and deep, then changes the angle and begins to hammer in and out of me in short, driving strokes.

My breasts bob and shake from the force of his thrusts and he rotates his hips, jockeying his knees underneath my thighs, allowing him to surge even deeper. He leans down and captures a nipple between his teeth and presses his thumb against my lips. "Suck it like it's my cock."

I do as he asks and swirl my tongue around his thumb, licking and sinking my teeth into his flesh.

Miles lets out a ragged groan, dropping his forehead to my neck as he pumps faster. Harder. Punishing. Exquisite. Fucking me how I've always wanted it. Hitting a spot deep inside me so expertly, I don't even know what to do with myself, so I grab his ass with my free hand and enjoy the ride as I suck like a maniac.

His tongue snakes out and licks a path under my jaw. "How am I doing?" He presses the fingers of his free hand low on my belly, increasing the friction so intensely, I suck in a breath. "Can you feel how deep I am?"

I'm so close to exploding, I can't answer. All I can do is moan, low and breathy as I clench around him.

"Soph?" He stills and shifts his face toward mine. "Are you okay? Talk to me. God, I'll stop—"

"Don't you dare." I release Miles's thumb and dig my nails into his ass. "I was about to come like a volcano. Or, I was, before you stopped."

He bellows with laughter which, probably inadvertently sends him deeper. "I'm sorry, let's get you there again."

Miles pulls out all the way and plunges back in, creating friction precisely where I need it. Again and again he moves inside me until I'm tightening around him, rocking into his thrusts and chasing my pleasure with complete and utter abandonment. He smashes his mouth against mine in a hungry, desperate kiss, sliding his tongue over mine.

"Finish me," I beg, encircling his cock with my fingers where it slips in and out of my body. "I'm so fucking close."

Without hesitation, Miles slides his finger along my clit and begins circling. Rotates his hips. We grind and thrust against each other's hands, our flesh slapping together in a frenzy. My pussy begins to quake and Miles drives home one final time. My orgasm explodes through my body, taking my sanity and consciousness and everything I thought I knew about life and turning it upside down.

He follows me with gasps and grunts, pumping his release into the condom. His hand rests on my hip for a while as we regain our equilibrium. Eventually, he pulls out, shedding the rubber before falling in bed next to me. Wrapping his arms around my belly, he presses his face into my hair and kisses my temple. "Incredible."

"*Incroyable.*" I turn in his embrace and rest my head against his chest.

Lying in Miles's arms, his heartbeat steady beneath my cheek, I can't help but wonder about fate.

How a single impulsive decision—to stay in Paris a little longer, to walk into a random wine bar—could lead me here, to this moment that feels both impossible and meant to be.

Of course as I close my eyes, wrapped in the quiet rhythm of his breathing, doubt creeps in.

What if this is just a fleeting moment for him? A Paris fling...

Should I let him stay with me tonight?

Or should I ask him to go?

Chapter Seven

WHAT HAPPENS NOW?

The room is quiet, except for the faint hum of the city beyond the window and the soft, steady sound of Sophie breathing beside me. She's still asleep, her body curled into mine, hand resting lightly on my chest. After the best sex of my life, I should feel content. Maybe even elated.

Instead, there's a knot tightening in my stomach. A small voice in my head whispering my biggest fear.

What if this meant more to me than it did to her?

Staring at the ceiling, I realize the early morning light now spills across the room in pale streaks. I can't stop replaying everything in my head. Meeting Sophie. Drinking wine. Our walk along the Seine. Discovering we were staying at the same hotel. The nightcap. Making love into the wee hours.

Last night was—hands down—the best time of my life. Unlike anything I've ever experienced. Every word, every touch, every look, every kiss felt like it unraveled something inside me I didn't even realize was tangled.

And yet, here I am, lying in the aftermath, feeling an old, familiar weight pressing down on me.

Though I try to hide it, I've always been good at second-guessing myself. Comes with the territory of being the gangly, nerdy kid growing up in my twin sister Shay's shadow. Shay was everything I wasn't—bright, popular, fearless. People gravitated toward her. She owned every room she walked into, while I was the one lurking in the corner. Playing computer games with my best friend. Hoping no one noticed me.

Even now, after building Hungry Llama, selling it for an absurd amount of money, and being able do whatever I want, there's still a part of me that feels like I don't belong. Lying here next to Sophie—this breathtaking, sophisticated, worldly woman—my old insecurities threaten to bubble to the surface all over again.

The truth is, I don't want to be just a moment for her. A charming distraction. Some guy she'll remember fondly someday, but not the one who fits into her real life.

Glancing at her, I watch the soft rise and fall of her shoulders. The way her thick, brown hair spills across the pillow. The peacefulness in her expression wasn't there when I met her. Could it be because of me?

God, I want to spend extra time with her. See where this could go. But I also don't want to overstay my welcome.

As if she knows I'm watching her, Sophie stirs and her eyelids flutter. I tense without meaning to. She shifts slightly, her gaze meeting mine. For a second, the warmth from the previous night flickers between us.

"Morning," she murmurs, husky with sleep.

"Morning," I reply, but the word comes too enthusiastic.

Awkward.

Sophie smiles but pulls back slightly, her hand slipping from my chest as she sits up, the covers pooling around her. A dusky pink nipple escapes and there's a beat of silence, like neither of us knows what to say. Yesterday morning she and I didn't know each other existed. Today, we've confided in each other some of our deepest secrets and I've been inside her body multiple times.

Yet, somehow the easiness we had seems distant now. Replaced by something fragile, uncertain.

I clear my throat, sitting up too, trying to fill the space. "I, uh... I hope I didn't snore."

"No." Sophie's smile remains pasted on her face, but I can't help but notice it doesn't quite extend to her eyes. She feels as unsure as I do. "After the dirty talk, you were quiet as a mouse."

Jeez.

Memories of all the filthy things I said to her when we were fucking flood my brain. I'm sure my face is as red as a beet. Sophie unleashed something in me and I became the man I always knew lived deep inside me. Doesn't mean I'm not feeling weird about it now.

Obviously. She and I are having the world's most uncomfortable morning-after dialogue.

Sophie settles back against the pillows and manages to cover her breast with the sheet. "Last night was..."

"Transcendent," I finish, and immediately second-guess my choice of words. I'm such a word nerd.

Her lips curve slightly into the genuine grin I'm falling for. "Yeah. I couldn't have put it better myself."

Relief washes over me, but it doesn't erase the questions swirling in my mind. Before I can stop myself, I blurt out, "Do you believe in fate?"

"Fate?" Sophie blinks, as though she's caught off guard.

"Yeah." I nervously run a hand through my hair, which must look like I've electrocuted myself. "You know, like...things happen for a reason. Sometimes you meet the perfect person at the right time. Woo-woo kind of stuff."

She leans back against the headboard, her expression thoughtful. "I used to think I didn't," she admits. "But, after meeting you...I don't know. Yesterday wasn't just chance. Fate is the word I thought about as I fell asleep."

Her words hit me deeper than I expect. I feel a flicker of hope this might continue today.

"What about you?" She tilts her head slightly.

I hesitate, then shrug. "I've never thought about it much. But meeting you is the kind of thing I can't chalk up to coincidence."

With our admissions, the tension in the room lifts.

"So," she says after a moment, pulling her knees up to her chest. "What happens next? For you, I mean. What's your plan?"

I let out a small laugh. "The million-dollar question. Or I guess, technically, the billion-dollar question."

She raises an eyebrow, amused.

"I don't have a plan." I shrug then lean back next to her. "I bought a one-way ticket to Europe, figured I'd wander for a while. See what happens."

"Wander where?" She rests her head on my shoulder.

"Honestly? No idea," I say. "I was kinda hoping Paris would point me in the right direction."

There's a glint of something playful in her eyes. "Well, you're in luck. Paris is very proficient at pointing people in the right direction."

"And you?" I ask *her* the million-dollar question. "What's next for you?"

Her smile falters slightly, and she glances down at her hands. "I'm heading to Bordeaux tomorrow."

"Sounds fun." I can hear the hesitation in my voice. "How long will you stay?"

"Oh, my plan was for a few weeks," she says quickly. "I was… It's complicated. My parents are wonderful and I haven't seen them in awhile. I know they worry about me more than they let on."

I nod, understanding completely. I have my own set of helicopter parents. Part of me wonders if she regrets having set plans. Does she want to spend time with me to see if what we have is real? On the other hand, I don't want to come across too aggressively.

"What if we spent today together?" I suggest before I can second-guess it.

She looks at me, surprised. "Really?"

"Yeah." I kiss her temple. "This is your city. Show me your favorite places. All the little spots tourists don't know about. You said Paris is good at pointing people in the right direction? Maybe it can do the same for both of us. Together."

Her eyes search mine, and for a moment, I wonder if I've pushed too far. But then she smiles and it feels like the sun is breaking through the clouds. "Yeah. Okay."

With our plan in place, all remnants of awkwardness melt away, replaced by the easy rhythm we found the previous night.

"Before we get up, though..." I nibble on her ear. "There's unlimited things to explore here in your bedroom."

Sophie giggles and turns my face toward hers. "Yeah, I think we may need at least another round."

Maybe it's not about having all the answers.

Maybe it's about letting things unfold, one moment at a time.

Chapter Eight

IT'S BEEN A PERFECT day.

Leading into a perfect night. Starting with dinner at my favorite hole-in-the wall restaurant, *L'Élan Secret*, an intimate spot close to our hotel with rustic charm and an air of mystery. I've been coming to for years. It doesn't bother with signs or Instagram. It's not romantic per se, the tables are close enough to eavesdrop. The waiters treat you like family.

Perfect for our final night together.

Or is it?

The glow of a candle flickers between us. Miles leans back in his chair, watching me with a curious, half-smiling expression he's worn since the moment we met.

"So." He tilts his wine glass just enough to swirl it. "What was your favorite part of today?"

I pause, pretending to think, though the answer is obvious. "Easy. The crêpes."

"You can't say the crêpes. You're cheating." His grin widens.

"They were perfect," I counter, smirking. "Fluffy, golden, perfectly drizzled Nutella. Miles, the crêpes carried the day."

He laughs. A soft, warm guffaw drawing a glance from the next table. "I mean, they were terrific," he leans forward, "but what about *Parc des Buttes-Chaumont*? The bridge? The views? You didn't stop talking about the light."

"Well, yeah. The light *was* stunning," I admit. "But it didn't beat the crêpes."

"You have your priorities straight," he teases, though his tone is laced with something heavier.

I take a sip of my wine, letting the silence stretch for a beat. Our day together replays in my mind like a film montage: wandering through a small art gallery hidden behind an ivy-covered door in the Marais, laughing at the tiny bookshop where he found a graphic novel so old it practically disintegrated in his hands, walking along the quiet canal as the late-afternoon sun rippled over the water.

The whole day could be a rom-com movie of the Paris I love most. The version that is effortlessly enchanting without even trying.

Studying him, I take in the way the candlelight softens his features. His messy hair and the strong lines of his jaw. There's an ease about him. It wasn't there earlier, but something else, too. A kind of weight he hasn't put into words.

"Okay." I set my glass down. "Your turn. What was *your* favorite part?"

His gaze fixes on me with amusement. "*Hmmm*. It's tough." He quirks a brow. "I mean, the crêpes were obviously life-changing."

"Obviously." I nod.

"But…" He hesitates, glancing over my shoulder and back at me. "I think it was walking with you along the canal. The stretch where it was quiet, just us. It was…perfect."

The way he says it makes my chest tighten, and I have to look away because it gives me all the feels. "It was."

The waiter passes, offering wine, but I shake my head. I've had enough. Miles waves him off too, resting his elbows on the table. For a moment, the conversation stalls, but it's not uncomfortable. It feels…easy. Like there's a ton of things unspoken between us and even though neither of us knows where to start, we'll get there.

I'm not used to this. The ease. The connection. With Mark, I was always on edge. Waiting for him to find another thing to be pissed at me about. It's been so long since I've let myself… *feel* anything like this. But is it real?

"So, you're heading to Bordeaux tomorrow," he says, addressing the elephant in the room. The clock is ticking.

"Yeah." I rest my chin on my palm.

He looks down at the tablecloth nervously. "How long will you stay?"

"I dunno, I want to spend some quality time with them," I admit. "They're great, but it depends. It can be...a lot."

He raises an eyebrow, waiting.

"They're worried I've fallen apart after my breakup, though it's been months now. I guess they still treat me like I'm a teenager half the time," I explain, laughing lightly. "Every decision I make is either a concern or a critique. Every visit turns into a long list of suggestions about what I should be doing with my life. They mean well, but..." I trail off, shrugging.

He nods, like he understands completely. "Parents are complicated."

"What about yours?" I tilt my head, studying him.

He runs his finger along the stem of his glass. "They're also great," he says conclusively. "But, yeah. Complicated. My dad was a professional hockey player—he's a force. Big, loud, larger than life. He wanted me to follow in his footsteps, but I never cared about sports the way he does."

"Never?" I'm not surprised, but when a parent wants you to do something it's not always your choice.

"Well, I didn't hate it." He shakes his head slightly. "I preferred staying inside, glued to a screen, designing worlds and playing games. My mom left me alone—she was busy with Shay and her beauty pageants—but my dad…" He pauses, his smile turning faintly self-deprecating. "Let's just say we didn't have a lot in common. Snowboarding was the closest I got to something he could relate to."

"And your sister?" I'm curious about his twin.

"Shay." His voice softens. "She's…incredible. She's been through the wringer and remains tough as hell. The thing is, when her epilepsy started getting bad in high school, all the family focus shifted to her. My parents hovered, worried, made everything about keeping her safe. I get it, but I kind of slipped through the cracks."

I continue to watch the way his fingers trace the edge of his glass. The way his voice tightens as he speaks. "Was it hard to be overlooked?"

"It was." He leans back. "At the same time, it also gave me room to figure things out on my own. And Austin—my best friend—kind of filled the gaps. We'd been gaming together forever and it led to us designing and dreaming up what eventually became Hungry Llama. We've been each other's anchor for nearly twenty years."

"And now?" I sense a slight hint of melancholy and I hate it.

"Well." He shrugs. "Now he's engaged to Shay. Our company's been sold, and...I don't know. Everything I built my life around has moved on except for me. I'm not *exactly* sad. I'm convinced the future holds something amazing. I just don't know what it is yet."

Wow. I can't even formulate a response. I feel a slight pang of doubt. Have I stepped into something bigger than I realized? Something I might not know how to handle?

Before I can dwell on it, the waiter returns with the check. Miles grabs his wallet before I can argue.

Outside, on the way back to the hotel, the air is cool and sweet, carrying the faint scent of flowers from the nearby park. The street lamps cast long shadows across the cobblestones. It feels like Miles and I have walked together like this for years and all my trepidation from a few moments ago disappears.

I don't want this to end.

The words tumble out before I can think them through. "You could come with me."

"To Bordeaux?" He stops in his tracks.

I nod a hair too vigorously. My cheeks heat up too. "It's beautiful in the spring," I blurt out. "And you don't have any plans, do you? It wouldn't be...weird, would it?"

"Weird, no. Bold, maybe." His lips twitch, like he's trying not to smile.

I wince. "Bold in a bad way?" I press, second-guessing myself.

"Sophie." He wraps his arms around me and presses a kiss to my forehead. "It's bold in the best way. But are you positive? I mean. Bordeaux. Your family. Me. You've known me for twenty-four hours. What will they think?"

"You wouldn't *have* to meet them." I wave my hand like I can erase the implication. "Unless you wanted to. I mean, I wouldn't... *force* anything. It's just..." I take a breath to steady myself before meeting his gaze. "I don't want this to end tomorrow. Not yet."

He studies me for a long moment. I can feel my stomach twisting as I wait for his response.

"Neither do I." He kisses my on the lips this time and the knot in my chest begins to loosen.

I pretend to pick a piece of lint off his jacket. "So...we'll figure it out?"

"We'll figure it out," he agrees. "I'll book a hotel. Make some separate plans so you have quality time with them. Whatever makes you comfortable. But I'm in."

Relief floods through me. "You're in? Are you some sort of masochist?"

"Apparently." He throws his head back and laughs with his whole being.

Holy shit. He's coming with me to Bordeaux.

As we continue our walk back, hand in hand, I let the worry drift away. For now, it's enough to just enjoy this moment.

I'm going to let myself believe in the possibility of something big between us.

Even if I know it's a long shot.

Chapter Nine

Having dinner with the parents of a woman I just met wasn't remotely on my radar when I decided to escape to Europe.

Forty-eight hours ago, I was some random guy in Paris, wandering through streets I didn't know, wondering what the hell I was doing in France.

Now I'm in Le Porge—a village outside of Bordeaux I'd never even heard of—where the air smells like salt and pine, and the sound of the Atlantic hums all around us.

It's wild, practically untouched. Sand dunes stretch to infinity. The trees whisper with the breeze. The village feels frozen in time—small, slow, deliberate. Earlier today, when she showed me around the town, Sophie moved through it like she's part of the place.

Two days ago, I didn't know her. Now, I can't take my eyes off her.

Dinner at Sophie's parents' house is nothing short of enchanting. The entire experience is warm, personal, and effortlessly welcoming.

This centuries-old home feels alive, like it's been nurtured by all the families who've lived here. Stone floors hold the memories of countless footsteps. Wooden beams overhead stretch across the ceilings like silent sentinels of time. Dumond family photos in mismatched frames, and bursts of vibrant color from Élise's floral arrangements decorate the space, giving it a lived-in, layered beauty.

The table is simple but perfect. A golden, roasted chicken sits in the center, surrounded by crispy rosemary potatoes and a fresh salad tossed. Bread, still warm from the *boulangerie*, is passed around, and a bottle of Bordeaux—likely from a nearby vineyard—seems to refill itself with Claude's gentle insistence.

Sophie sits close enough next to me, her elbow brushes mine now and then. Each small touch sends a spark through me, and I can't stop thinking how I can't remember life before I met her.

It's hard to believe how quickly things have moved.

Two nights ago, we traded witty banter after she spilled a glass of wine and it ended up being the most transformative, passionate night of my life. By yesterday, it was more. *Much* more.

Not just chemistry. Something deeper—something huge and terrifying and completely inevitable. When we woke up this morning, tangled together in the soft light of her hotel room, I could hardly believe how natural it felt. Like we'd been waking up together forever.

Our desire for each other is intense. Deep. Soulful. Not frenzied emulate-a-porn-video gymnastics. No, it's so much better. Sex with Sophie is like finding the missing page in a book I've been reading my whole life.

We left Paris midmorning. The train ride to Bordeaux was quiet, but not awkward. Sophie read most of the way, her hair catching the sunlight as it streamed through the window. The entire trip, I couldn't stop stealing glances at her. She always caught me, smirking faintly like she knew what I was thinking but didn't mind.

Now, sitting here in her parents' home, I'm overwhelmed by a strange, profound sense of belonging. It's a little unnerving, if I'm honest.

Sophie's dad, Claude's voice pulls me out of my thoughts. "So, Miles." He leans back in his chair, glass of wine in one hand. "You're from Seattle?"

"Yes." I set my fork down, trying to remember my manners. "Born and raised."

"And what brings you to France?" Élise's tone is curious but kind.

I glance at Sophie, who offers me a small, encouraging smile. "It was kind of a spur-of-the-moment decision. I sold my company and once things settled, I realized I didn't have anything tying me down for the first time in years. So, I booked a one-way ticket to Paris."

"An excellent choice. Paris is always a terrific idea." Claude raises his glass approvingly.

I laugh. "At least it's what I told myself. Though I didn't have a set plan. My whole day consisted of getting lost in a city where I don't speak the language. The epitome of bumbling American."

"Until you met Sophie," Élise says with a sly smile.

I feel the heat creep up my neck. "Uh, yeah. Yep."

"Mom!" Sophie shakes her head.

Claude thoughtfully takes a sip of wine. "You mentioned selling a company. What kind of work were you in?"

"I cofounded a gaming company with my best friend, Austin," I explain. "We made casual games—stuff you can play on your phone or tablet. Our biggest hit was called *Puzzle Pet Paradise*. It took off faster than we expected and we ended up growing the company into something much bigger than we'd ever dreamed possible."

"So you're taking time off?" Élise quirks a brow.

Inadvertently, I sigh. "Uh...yeah. I guess so."

"It's always important to have mental space to figure out what's next." Claude nods as if he understands completely.

"Yeah. Though it's strange after working so hard." I fidget with my napkin a bit. "I guess I need to figure out what I want to do in this next chapter."

As the conversation flows, I learn about Sophie's family story. I knew she was born in Paris, but Claude fills in some details about how they ended up in the US.

"I fell in love with an American." Élise serves herself another helping of salad. "We met while he was traveling in Paris."

Claude chuckles. "I was young and reckless. No plan, no direction—just wandering Europe, trying to 'find myself.' I met Élise at a café, and, well…" He shrugs like the rest is obvious.

"I was working as a waitress," Élise says in her charming accent. "And he could hardly order coffee. He asked me out, but I rejected him of course. He kept coming back. Every day for a week. Eventually, I gave in and we went on a date."

"Six weeks later, we were married," Claude finishes, grinning.

I'm visibly shocked. "Six weeks?"

"When you know, you know." Claude wraps his arm around his wife. "Why waste time?"

They laugh, and Élise pats his hand affectionately. "We stayed in Paris for a while, but when Sophie was born, Claude's work moved us to the US. We ended up in New York until a few years ago."

"You put up with it." Sophie leans against her mother but looks at me. "Mom hated the cold."

"It was unbearable." Élise shudders dramatically. "When Claude retired a few years ago, I insisted we come back to France. Paris is too expensive, but here outside of Bordeaux felt like the perfect place to settle."

I glance at Sophie who watches her parents with a mixture of fondness and quiet amusement. "Now they can't stop reminding me how much better life is here than in New York."

"Because it is." Claude ruffles her hair. "Though I'll admit, the US has its charms."

"It does, there's nowhere else like NYC." Sophie gazes at her dad fondly.

After a pause, Claude's eyes flick back to me. "So, Miles." He taps the table with his finger. "What about you? Any great love stories in your past?"

Here we go. The interrogation.

I shake my head. "Nope. I spent my twenties building my company. No time for a nerdy computer geek like me. But, then my best friend got engaged to my twin sister, so I think I caught a bug."

"Only a nerd would liken me to a bug." Sophie smirks, nudging me with her elbow.

I'm pretty sure my face is as red as a tomato.

Claude chortles. "Well, you seem to have a forgiving heart, my sweetheart."

The air shifts slightly. Probably because the three of them are recalling Sophie's previous relationship. Sophie ducks her head, focusing a little too intently on her plate. I don't know what to say. She was coming here to spend time with them because they thought she was brokenhearted.

Instead, she brought me.

I don't know how to put a label on whatever this is between us yet—but I can't ignore how much the comment stirs something deep in my chest. I'd never do anything to hurt Sophie. If we were together I'd cherish each day. Each hour. Each minute. Each second.

Élise looks pointedly at me. "You seem like a very kind man, Miles. And a respectable one. I hope you'll enjoy Bordeaux."

"I already am." I can't help but to glance at Sophie.

As dinner winds down, the conversation drifts to other topics—Claude's workshop. Élise's favorite florist. The best bakeries in the area.

To me, though, Claude's earlier words linger long after the plates are cleared and the laughter has faded.

When you know, you know.

I wonder if it could be so simple.

Chapter Ten

I WAKE UP TO the steady sound of Miles breathing.

My cheek rests on his chest as the initial vestiges of morning light filter through the curtains into the room. I feel safe here, wrapped up in him. His warmth anchoring me to the moment.

Miles smells like clean soap, cedar, and a hint of salt from the ocean air—comforting and familiar, with a trace of leather and citrus.

I decide to keep my eyes closed. Stretch this quiet bubble of time just a little longer. I notice something's off, though. Miles's breathing is steady, but there's tension in the rise and fall of his chest—like he's somewhere else entirely.

When I'm ready, I tilt my head up to find him staring at the ceiling, brows slightly furrowed, lost in thought.

"Morning." I stroke his nipple gently until it puckers.

He glances down at me, forcing a smile that doesn't quite reach his eyes. "Morning."

My heart pinches at how far away he looks. Like he's here, but not really. "You're quiet. Is there something wrong? Did my parents scare the shit out of you?"

"No. Well..." For a moment, I think he's going to brush it off, but instead, he lets out a slow breath and rubs his hand over his face. "I've been thinking about something I did a while ago."

"Oh?" I prop myself up on my elbow.

He hesitates, like the words are heavy and he's not certain he should let them out. Eventually, he glances at me, his eyes raw and uncertain. "Have you ever said something you regret? Something making you wonder if you're even capable of not screwing up the things that matter?"

The gritty honesty in his voice catches me off guard, but I nod. "Yeah. Of course. I think everyone has."

"God." He exhales again, his thumb tracing absently over my shoulder. "It's about Shay and Austin. When I found out they were together, I didn't handle it well."

He doesn't say anything else at first. It's almost like he's wading through the memory and picking his words carefully.

"I said things to her I can't take back about things she can't control. She's my twin. I love her more than anything, and I still managed to hurt her." His gaze fixes somewhere past me. "I mean, we're all good now. I think. Sure, I lashed out because I was scared. I didn't know how to deal with the thought of losing her. Of losing Austin, too. They're the two people I'm closest to and it felt like they lied to me when they got together. Shut me out. I was so afraid of being left behind, I didn't realize how much damage I was doing."

I watch him carefully as he speaks. How his expression shifts between regret and something deeper—making my heart ache for him.

"I thought I was protecting her," he continues. "But I was just protecting myself. I didn't get it. I didn't understand what it meant to care about someone so much you'd risk everything for them. I thought they were being reckless, but the truth is...they *knew*. They knew what they felt, and they chose each other."

Miles turns to look at me, his eyes holding mine like he's searching for—reassurance, maybe? Understanding. "I didn't get it until now. Until *you*."

His words unravel something inside me I didn't know was wound so tight. My heart stutters and I feel my pulse race as the weight of what he's saying sinks in.

For a moment, neither of us speaks. I can see how hard this is for him. How much it took to let me see this part of him. I grip his hand, lacing my fingers through his and squeeze gently.

"You're not going to hurt me, Miles." I trace the scruff on his chin with my free hand. "I know you won't."

His lips twitch like he wants to believe me but doesn't quite know how. "I don't want to mess this up," he whispers against my ear. "Whatever this is. Sophie, it feels huge. I want to be worthy of it. Of you."

The vulnerability in his voice makes my chest tighten, and I lean in, brushing my lips against his. Our kiss is slow and soft. A promise as much as a kiss. When we pull back, I let my forehead rest against his.

"You are," I whisper. "You already are."

"Fucking hell, do you know what you do to me?" Miles growls as he moves over me, each muscle flexing with his movement.

He places one leg between mine against my core, cups my breast and kisses me like we didn't spend all night making love. I have no shame in grinding against him, whimpering when the stimulation to my clit sends zings up my spine. "Oh, Miles. *Yessss.*"

"You're so fucking perfect." He kisses down my neck to my collarbone. "I can't keep my hands to myself. Your body is what dreams are made of."

I dig my fingers into his scalp, pulling him closer to me. "The things you do to my body are what dreams are made of, silly. For the record, I have an IUD and haven't needed condoms in a very long time. If you feel safe with me, we can skip the condoms."

"I'm clean too, I promise. I'd never hurt you, baby." He snarls wolfishly, and the irony isn't lost on me.

I nod and grind against him again, soaking his leg but making us both sigh in anticipation of what's next. Miles sucks my nipple between his lips, then nips it. Does the same with the other one. Alternates sucking and biting them until they're stiff and red. My hands work their way down to his cock. He's rock hard and I love his deep gasp when I stroke him from root to tip.

My hips officially have a mind of their own, circling and pulsing as we grind together. He's not even inside me yet, and I feel like I'm on the edge of splintering into pieces. He bites the skin above my breast and smiles up at me as he shifts position to nudge my opening with his shaft, framing my face in his hands. "I love to see your face when I sink inside you."

My breath hitches when he presses just the tip inside, waiting for me to adjust to him. "You're *everything*."

"No, *you* are." He pushes in farther. "You feel so damn incredible."

"I can't believe *how* incredible sex with you is," I agree as he buries himself balls-deep inside me and I grip both of his ass cheeks and flex around him and he cringes.

He grips my cheeks. "I keep telling you, if you keep your sexy little trick up this'll go way faster than either of us want."

I repeat the motion. "You've not disappointed me yet."

"Shit," he mutters and then begins to move. Slow and steady, but I grip his ass and hitch my thighs a bit higher, and we both lose it. He picks up the speed and I hang on for dear life as my orgasm builds, shooting through me and leaving me a complete noodle. Miles joins me, blurting out my name before collapsing next to me.

His hand slides up to cup my face as he kisses me again—deeper. Sweeter. Like he's trying to tell me everything he can't quite say.

When we eventually break apart, I brush my fingers along his jaw. "My parents were spot-on, you know. I don't think this kind of connection happens by accident."

"I don't think so either." He wraps his arm around me.

For a moment, we just stare at each other, the air between us charged but steady. It's strange how someone can come into your life and feel like they've always been there, like they were just waiting to be found.

"So," I say. "Where do we go next?"

The boyish smile I'm starting to love tugs at his lips. "Wherever you want."

"Cool." I settle back against him. "Because I don't want this to end yet."

"Me neither." He pulls me closer.

I close my eyes and let the steady rhythm of his breathing calm me.

Who knows what the next few weeks will look like.

Funny thing is, I'm not afraid to find out.

Chapter Eleven

Funny how ironic life is.

I never thought I'd be the guy who brings the girl home to meet his family. Yet here I am, standing in Austin's ridiculous, expensive high-rise condo, looking out at Puget Sound while my parents laugh in the next room. My sister Shay pours wine like it's a competitive sport, though she doesn't drink herself.

Sophie sits at the center of it all, a little flushed but charming as ever.

I'm both calm and nervous as hell.

"Looks like she's handling your folks better than you ever did." Austin hands me a beer. He watches Sophie with a mix of amusement and approval, which I expected.

"She's much better at this than I am." I beam at her despite myself.

Sophie glances my way from where she's perched between Shay and my mom on the couch. They're all laughing at some ridiculous story—probably about me as a teenager. I don't even want to know.

"Shay's adding fuel to the fire, by the way," I grumble.

Austin shrugs. "What are twin sisters for?"

"Support," I say dryly.

He slugs me in the arm. "Where's the fun in that?"

It's been three months since Sophie and I stood on the edge of the Seine, fumbled our way through figuring out what "this" was or wasn't, and decided to give it a shot. Somehow, through train rides, cheap wine, incredible sunsets, unbelievable sex and so many laughs, we made it here. Back to Seattle.

Together.

"Okay, Miles, enough stalling." Shay motions me over. "You're not getting out of this. You promised stories."

I smirk. "You just want to hear about the time I nearly broke my ankle so you can torment me forever."

"*Obviously*. She settles deeper into the couch. "Dad wants the travel recap because he's decided you've been 'squandering your youth,' despite the fact you could buy a small country at thirty."

From the armchair, my dad—Goran Stojanović, the hockey legend himself—raises his hands in mock innocence. "No need to rest on your laurels."

"Don't pretend you're not dying to hear about all the places your son fell on his face." My mom, Annika, nudges him with her elbow.

Sophie stifles a laugh with the back of her hand and it pulls my attention to her like a magnet. She's radiant—flushed cheeks, dark sweater falling off one shoulder in the effortlessly elegant way she has. When our eyes meet, for a moment, I forget anyone else is in the room.

"Ahem." Austin smacks my back with the palm of his hand. "Less ogling. More words."

"Fine, fine." I lean against the fireplace, my beer dangling from my hand. "I'll give you the highlight reel of Europe. Keep in mind, Sophie's the organized one. She had a camera bag, an itinerary, and the magical ability to navigate every train system we encountered. I mostly carried our bags and smiled like an idiot."

"Sounds accurate." Sophie nods and purses her lips playfully.

Everyone laughs, and I shake my head. "*Anyway*. The trip started in Paris, obviously. Sophie took me to all her secret spots—places you won't find on Instagram or in guidebooks. Like a little café in Montmartre that served croissants so delicious I actually got emotional."

"*Emotional*," Shay scoffs disbelievingly. "Like, *tears*?"

I fix her with a mock pointed glare. "Uh, *yeah*. You had to be there."

"Then I ruined it by dragging him to the flea market," Sophie chimes in. "Miles thought I was trying to ditch him in the middle of nowhere."

"Okay, in my defense," I point at her, "it was *huge*. Rows and rows of stalls. I lost her twice and panicked both times. Also, someone tried to sell me a 19th-century chamber pot."

This earns another round of laughter, even from my dad. Sophie shakes her head at me and points to the floor by the front door. "Instead, you bought a weird leather satchel."

"It's *vintage*," I argue. "It has character."

"It smells like mothballs, the whole place stinks now," Shay mutters.

"Moving on," I say cursorily. "From Paris, we went to Switzerland. I convinced Sophie to snowboard with me in Zermatt."

"And?" my mom prompts, leaning in.

"She's a ringer," I pout. "I found out she's been boarding since she was five years old. She's way better than I am."

Sophie rolls her eyes, but I catch the way she's holding back a smile. "Not true. I didn't want to hurt your fragile ego."

I move toward her, unable to stay away. "You were graceful. I fell into a snowbank and disappeared for a full minute."

Dad—ever the athlete—lets out a booming laugh and points at Sophie. "Tell me you got all of this on camera."

"Oh, you know I did," Sophie says proudly. "It's my favorite video of the trip."

"Traitor," I grumble, though I can't help but kiss her temple. "Then there was Italy," I continue. "Cinque Terre was my favorite town. We stayed in Vernazza in an Airbnb built into the cliffs where the streets are basically stairs. I still don't know how Sophie found the place but it had a balcony overlooking the ocean. We had the best meal of my life—pesto pasta, fresh fish caught an hour before it was served and tiramisu I'm still dreaming about."

"Well, you're conveniently leaving out the best part," Sophie adds. "Miles got seasick on the boat ride earlier in the day, once food was involved he had a miraculous recovery."

I groan. "You don't need to tell them *everything*."

"Oh, I won't. Clearly, we can't tell your parents about when you dropped trou—"

I cover her mouth with my palm. "You wouldn't."

Sophie laughs and even Shay looks impressed. "Wow, Stodge." She drums her fingers on the back of the couch. "This whole 'world traveler' thing suits you. Who knew?"

"I didn't," I admit. "And yet, somehow, it worked."

Sophie tilts her head, amused. "Stodge?"

I groan, shooting Shay a look. "Seriously? You had to bring my nickname up?"

From the armchair, Dad nods his approval, clearly enjoying this. "It's a solid name. Earned it myself on the ice, passed it down fair and square."

I roll my eyes but can't help smiling. "Yeah, well, it made sense back then. It's always been a part of me, but now..." I glance at Sophie. "Now it feels like it belongs to another version of me. One I'm ready to leave behind."

Sophie's smile is gentle, understanding. "You'll always be Miles to me."

Dad grunts in approval, raising his glass. "Smart woman. She's a keeper."

"Agreed." Mom is downright charmed. "What was your favorite country?"

"Spain," I say, grinning. "Barcelona, specifically. Sophie dragged me to the Picasso Museum."

"And you loved it," she says smugly.

"I did." I shrug. "It was...inspiring. But, we ended up at this hidden tapas bar down a side alley where no one spoke English. We sat at the bar, ate whatever they put in front of us, and drank wine straight from the porron."

Shay raises a brow. "What's a *porron*?"

"It's this glass thing." I gesture vaguely. "You have to pour the wine straight into your mouth without spilling. I failed spectacularly."

"You looked like a kid drinking out of a garden hose." Sophie shakes her head.

The memory makes me smile. I can still see her there, laughing so hard she cried, her face flushed and radiant under the soft glow of string lights. I clear my throat, feeling everyone's eyes on me. "Greece was a close second. Santorini."

"Oh, I've always wanted to go there." My mom's face lights up.

"It's as beautiful as you'd imagine." My gaze catches Sophie's again as I remembered the long, languid mornings making love in our hotel overlooking the sea. "The sunsets there are unreal—gold and pink, like something out of a painting. Every night we sat on the roof of this little restaurant, eating moussaka, drinking wine, and watching the sun sink into the Aegean."

I don't add it was the night I confessed I was completely, hopelessly in love with her and she reciprocated my feelings. I don't need to. Sophie looks at me and I know she remembers it, too.

"And now you're home." My dad squints at me.

"Yeah," I say, my throat a little tight, because I haven't told any of my family New York is going to be my new home. After Sophie's photography exhibit, I've decided to extend my break and study art for a couple of years. Travel with Sophie to her photo shoots.

Anyway, there's an even bigger announcement to make.

For a moment, the room is quiet—comfortable, but content.

My mom breaks the silence. "We're so happy you're happy, Miles. And, Sophie, we adore you."

"Thank you." Sophie reddens, like she's a little shy. "Your support means a lot."

And I can't wait another second. I hold out a hand to Sophie. "Come here for a second, my love."

"What are you doing?" She quirks a brow and slips her hand into mine.

"You'll see." I tug her gently to her feet and keep her close as we turn back to face my family. Sophie gives me a look—half-curious, half-nervous—but she doesn't pull away. I clear my throat, my fingers laced tightly through hers. "So, uh...there's something else we should tell you."

All eyes snap to us. Austin folds his arms. Shay's glass hovers midair. My mom's brows lift, and Dad leans forward like he's watching the final seconds of a tied game. I squeeze Sophie's hand and glance at her. There's a beautiful mix of nerves and excitement lighting up her face.

"Sophie and I…" I pause for just a beat, grinning like a lovesick fool. "The thing is, we're engaged. I asked her to marry me and she said yes."

The room goes deadly still—just long enough for Sophie to shoot me a *you're doing this now?* look—before everything explodes at once.

"Engaged?! Oh my *God*!" Mom gasps and claps her hands together, practically launching out of her chair.

Shay shrieks and almost trips over her own feet as she races toward us. "Are you serious?!" she yells, throwing her arms around Sophie. "This is the best news ever!"

Dad, bless him, lumbers to his feet slowly, a proud smile spreading across his face as he walks over and claps me on the shoulder. "My boy," he says gruffly, because it's how he always talks. "You've got a keeper."

Austin raises his beer in salute. "About time, Stodge. I always knew you were smart enough to lock down a gem."

Amid the chaos, I look at Sophie—her cheeks flushed and smile radiant as my mom practically smothers her in congratulations. My chest feels like it might burst.

"Was this your plan all along?" she whispers a few seconds later, tilting her head up at me as Shay drags her into another hug.

"Nope." I kiss her temple. "Couldn't keep it to myself. Let's tell your folks tomorrow."

"Welcome to the family, Sophie!" Dad booms.

Sophie shakes her head, her eyes shimmering with forever. "Thank you. I guess there's no turning back now."

"There isn't." I tug her close to my side. "I love you, Sophie and I can't wait to spend my life with you."

She smiles, her voice steady and full of certainty. "I love you too."

When her lips meet mine, it feels like stamping the final boarding pass to a life we've both been waiting for—a journey we'll take together from this moment on.

As my family's laughter fills the room, chaotic and full of love, I realize this isn't just the end of a chapter—it's the start of *everything*.

Sophie's not just a part of my story; she's the heart of it.

Wherever we go, whatever paths we take, I know one thing for sure.

With her by my side, I'll always be home.

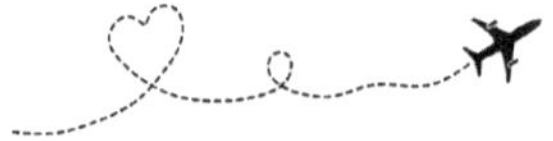

Thank you for reading *Boarding Pass*.
If Miles and Sophie swept you off your feet, I'd love if you left a quick review: *Leave your review here*

Up next! A first-class flight to Barcelona with two strangers, one spark, and no room to hide.
Preorder *First Class Fling* to fall for Santiago and Rosa:
Grab it here

Curious where Miles first showed up? Continue reading for a peak into the The Flirt Alert

Want more behind-the-scenes moments, sneak
peeks, and exclusive content?
Join my newsletter and never miss an update.

Behind the Scenes
Boarding Pass

I'M SO EXCITED TO share a little bit about the inspiration behind *Boarding Pass*. This story is all about taking risks, stepping outside your comfort zone, and finding something—or someone—you didn't even know you were looking for.

I've always had a passion for travel and experiencing new cultures. There's something magical about the way different places make you feel, how they bring out different sides of you. That's a big part of why I wanted to write this book—to explore what happens when two people, each at a crossroads in their lives, come together in a place where anything feels possible.

The idea for *Boarding Pass* also came from a moment in my own life—a chance encounter that changed everything. I won't give away all the details, but let's just say it started with an unexpected meeting and turned into the love of my life. That fleeting inspiration got me thinking about how serendipitous love can be, how it finds you when you least expect it, and how it's often tied to stepping outside your bubble.

Miles and Sophie's story is really special to me. They're two people who are a little lost in their own ways, but they find something extraordinary in each other. From the streets of Paris to the vineyards of Bordeaux, I wanted their journey to feel vibrant and real, like you're right there with them. It's a romance about risk, discovery, and that electric spark that changes everything.

I hope *Boarding Pass* gives you all the feels and maybe inspires you to chase your own adventures. You never know what's waiting for you just around the corner—or across an ocean. Thanks for being part of this journey with me!

The Flirt Alert – Chapter One

What the actual fuck?

It's scarcely November and it's snowing in Seattle. From my corner office, I watch thousands of fluffy flakes drift in lazy spirals to the pavement fifteen stories below. We rarely get winter weather in the city. Never this early in the year.

Though it's nearing eight a.m., the sidewalks and streets are practically empty. The city shuts down at the slightest hint of snow and today is no different, leaving downtown almost quiet and peaceful. Unfortunately, the turmoil in my mind churns like the froth on my extra-hot, double tall vanilla latte, which is cooling on my desk.

I'm about to get my day started when I notice a woman wearing a bright-pink coat and matching beanie with ridiculously high heels stop at the entrance to the building. She looks up at the sky, sticks out her tongue and whirls around in a circle with her arms outstretched like a little kid.

God, to be so carefree. Too bad she's going to break an ankle in this weather.

"Austin, bro, you're gonna love this!" Miles Stojanović, aka Stodge, my best friend and business partner in our multimillion-dollar casual gaming company, Hungry Llama, barrels into my office like a tornado. He holds a snowboard in one hand and shoves a brochure at me with the other. "Executive retreat booked at Crystal Mountain. Look at this place. There are rooms to hold meetings and team building exercises. Lodging is onsite. Good food. Solitude so we can focus. I've even reserved the Summit House at the top of the mountain for a send-off dinner. Plus, if people want to ski or snowboard, it will be perfect."

Stodge's enthusiasm always puts me in a fantastic mood. It's infectious; exactly like his passion for the business we started in college. He's a creative genius, friend to all and the heart of Hungry Llama. I'm the numbers and operations guy who largely stays behind the scenes. Our opposite strengths have made us unstoppable in the gaming world. The past eight years have been an incredible ride.

"Yeah, it checks all the basic boxes." I lean against my desk and study the brochure. The thought of being trapped on a mountain isn't appealing at all. "How much is it going to cost? We're there for business, not to have fun."

Miles drops the snowboard and makes himself at home in my DXRacer Master gaming chair. "Dude. You've got to lighten up. We're gonna gross close to a billion dollars this year. Puzzle Pet Paradise is crushing." He leans forward. "The team is exhausted. Showing them how much we appreciate them is equally as important as the day-to-day shit."

"Day to day *shit*, eh?" I flip through the glossy pictures of the resort's proposed schedule and menu while my business partner spins around in my chair, full of childlike joy that always seems to bubble up no matter what the situation. It kinda reminds me of pink-coat girl on the street from earlier.

He shakes his head slowly like I'm killing his vibe. "Dude, seriously. Loosen the fuck up. We all need a little AFK time."

"I'm not saying no. I'm reminding you we have bigger issues to solve." The truth is, Miles and I have a key role to fill at the company. "We need to hire a Marketing and Events executive like...yesterday."

"Already done." Stodge comes to a full stop and drums his knuckles on the armrest. Looks me in the eye, then averts his gaze.

Jesus. His impulsiveness. "What. Did. You. Do?"

"You can't get mad." He holds up his hands defensively. "Let me explain..."

I bridge my fingers across my nose. "*Stodge*..."

"Fine. I'll rip off the bandage. I...I offered the job to Shay." Miles cowers like I'm about to lob my keyboard at him.

The room grows as cold as the winter storm outside my window. *Shay Stojanović*. His twin sister. A she-devil. My chest tightens as memories from my past bubble up like acid. The mere mention of her name gives me hives. Being around her every day? *Fuck* no.

"Your sister?" I choke out, my voice rising. "VP of Marketing and Events? Has she ever held a *job*, Stodge?"

Miles shifts uncomfortably, still avoiding my eyes. "She's got the appropriate experience and gave me the idea for the retreat. More importantly, she's my family and needs a break."

"Not at the company you and I have built together. No way. Not a fucking chance," I snap. This is the ultimate betrayal. "You *know* how I feel about her, Miles."

"I do. But I don't quite understand why something that happened nearly a decade ago needs to define you." He's quiet now as he rubs his chin thoughtfully. "I mean, it was high school. Can't you let it go?"

Easy for him to say. I get up and stare out the window again. The snowstorm is all but over, save one or two straggler flakes. Thinking about that fateful day makes it hard for me to breathe. What Shay did still haunts me.

I don't see any reason to let it go. "You weren't there."

"Thank fucking God I wasn't or I'd have killed you both. I told you she was going through some, eh...stuff. We were *kids*. Do you truly *still* hate her?" Miles doesn't understand. He doesn't have a mean bone in his body. He's a live-and-let-live kind of guy. Things roll off his back.

For me? Not so much.

I squeeze my eyes shut and try to push the memories away. "Yeah, I do. I can't explain it except to say, with all due respect, she's the complete opposite of you and there's no way I'm entrusting her with such a big role at my company."

"Uh...*our* company. And sorry, that's not good enough." There's a note of stubborn determination in his voice that I recognize. He rarely plays the card, but when he does...yeah. Stodge isn't letting this go.

I try another tactic. "Marketing isn't a remote job. We need someone who's in Seattle—who can come into the office every day."

"I'm well aware." He leans so far back in the chair I'm afraid it's going to fall over. "Trust me on this. I know Shay is my twin but after things ended with Devon, she was forced to move back to Seattle. I promise you, she's a great fit for the company. She needs this job and I'm asking you to get on board. If it doesn't work out, I'll take full responsibility."

The raw sincerity in his eyes makes me feel trapped. Hires of this magnitude are ordinarily unanimous decisions. We've worked too hard to build Hungry Llama into a gaming juggernaut to fuck things up for a favor to his sister. It sucks balls that I don't have a choice but to see how this plays out.

"Look. Since you already offered her the job without even mentioning it to me, my condition is simple. I can't—won't—work with her directly. She'll report to you." I cross my arms defiantly.

He runs his fingers through his hair. "Austin, *no*. I supervise hundreds of remote employees on the development and creative teams. You manage the entire executive team. Besides, having my twin sister report to me? That's *weird*."

"Do you seriously think Shay's going to respect my position? She's a spoiled princess. The ultimate mean girl. Someone who chases status not substance. If she weren't your twin, there's an excellent chance I'd fire her before she logs into her computer." I stand and pound my fist on the desk.

Miles leaps from the chair and squares up to me. "For fuck's sake. We're grown-ass adults. Shay has never said a bad word about you. Do you think you may have blown things out of proportion? We've all changed dramatically since high school. Can't you give her a chance?"

I shake my head, a cold certainty settles in my stomach. I never told Miles the whole story. "*No*."

There's a long silence where Stodge and I stare at each other with eyes narrowed. Even at our most competitive, the two of us don't fight. Ever. If he pushes this any further I'm afraid our record won't remain intact.

Eventually he speaks, his voice heavy with resignation. "Fuck it. If you run into issues, I promise you won't have to interact with her."

"Thanks." I feel a hollow ache in my chest, knowing that I may have won this battle but in all likelihood, I'll lose the war.

Stodge is deflated. "Uh…yeah. Sure." He picks up his snowboard and stands at the door, presumably waiting for me to say something else.

When I remain stoic and silent, he slips out without waving. The door clicks shut behind him, leaving me alone to stew about the situation at hand. I was a kid with a load of brains, a shitty home life, and zero social skills. I was also hopelessly smitten with my best friend's sister, who happened to be the most popular girl at school.

She ruthlessly chewed me up and spit me out without a second thought. Miles wasn't there to witness it because he was otherwise…occupied. The aftermath could have ended our friendship, but Shay moved away so… Anyway, seeing Shay again is going to suck but I can't let the situation fuck things up with Miles.

I'm smart enough to know if it comes down to it, he'll always choose his twin sister.

You can't change who your family is. I live with this sad truth every fucking day.

Goddammit.

Oh, I know it's been years and I should forgive and forget and all that.

Revenge sounds better, though.

Yeah. Much better.

I should be a bigger person. I'm no longer a scrawny, insecure geek. I've built Hungry Llama into one of the hottest companies in the world. I'm not hurting for cash. I own several properties. I have no problem getting laid. I'd like to think I'm a decent boss. I support a ton of philanthropic causes.

So why can't I let it go?

Because I want to bring her down a notch.

Yep. That's it. I want to give her a taste of her own medicine.

I'll let Miles know I've changed my mind and Shay can report to me. Then I'll be an asshole. Not any asshole, a *subtle* asshole. Take great pleasure in making her life miserable until she quits on her own accord. That way I'll get rid of her and keep my friendship with Miles intact.

I stand at the window.

It's snowing again. Everything is quiet.

The world might look peaceful from up here, but I know better.

A storm is beginning, and I'm standing directly in its path.

She ruined him once. Now she works for him. Read The Flirt Alert

Acknowledgments

Cover Design: Kate Farlow Y'all. That Graphic.

Editor: Grace Bradley Editing, LLC

Formatting: Willow Yanarella

PR: Dani Sanchez Wildfire Marketing

Literary Agent: Stephanie Phillips, SBR Media

Website Maven: Sherri Kiarsis, Ruby Moon Designs

My Right Hand: Willow Yanarella

YAY to Kaylene's Backstage Krew, my wonderful ARC Team!

Dedication

FOR MY IRISH SOULMATE,

To the man I met on a chance encounter in an Irish pub on Paddy's Day—thank you for proving that love at first sight isn't just for stories. Every day with you is its own adventure, and I'm forever grateful for that night, that pub, and the twist of fate that brought us together.

This one's for you.

Always.

About the Author

Kaylene Winter is a best-selling author of steamy, contemporary romance.

Each character-driven novel is filled with snappy dialogue, pop-culture references and enough steam to make you fan yourself. Kaylene weaves authenticity, emotion and angst into a turbulent rollercoaster ride of love, passion and soul-searing romance always ending with a delicious HEA.

Kaylene lives in Seattle with her amazing Irish husband and her Pomsky, Phalen. She loves creating art of all kinds.

Other Titles

Find Me Everywhere

www.kaylenewinter.com/links